Ms. Frizzle's Adventures
ANCIENT EGYPT

Ms. Frizzle's Adventures
ANCIENT EGYPT

For information regarding permis-
sion, write to Scholastic Inc.,
Attention: Permissions Department,
557 Broadway, New York, NY 10012.
• ISBN 0-590-44681-9 • Text copyright
© 2001 by Joanna Cole. Illustrations
copyright © 2001 by Bruce Degen. All rights
reserved. Published by Scholastic Inc.
MS. FRIZZLE'S ADVENTURES, THE MAGIC
SCHOOL BUS, SCHOLASTIC, and associated
logos are trademarks and/or registered trademarks
of Scholastic Inc. • 12 11 10 9 8 7 6 5 4 3 2 1   2 3 4 5 6
7/0 • Printed in the U.S.A.   08   •   First   Scholastic
paperback printing, September 2002 • The text type was set
in 15-point Gill Sans. The illustrator used pen and ink, water-
color, color pencil, and gouache for the paintings in this book.

The author thanks Magy and Mona, her tour guides in Egypt.
The author and illustrator would like to thank Dr. Phyllis Saretta, an Egyptologist who
lectures at the Metropolitan Museum of Art, for her careful review of the manuscript and illustrations.

It was a long flight.
When night came, everyone fell asleep.
Well, *almost* everyone.

As the sun rose, we found ourselves flying over Egypt.
Down below, we saw the Nile River.
Green farms ran along either side of the river.
Beyond the farms, there was nothing but desert.
It was sand, sand, sand, as far as the eye could see.

Sure enough, something interesting did happen.
As our feet reached the ground,
the cars and trucks disappeared.
So did the modern people.
Even the horses and camels were gone.
We were back in ancient Egypt.
I can't imagine how that happened. Can you?

IN THE AGE OF PYRAMIDS, THERE WERE NO CAMELS OR HORSES IN EGYPT. THEY CAME LATER.

THERE WERE NO TOURISTS FROM THE 21ST CENTURY, EITHER.

WE CAME LATER, TOO.

EGYPT IN ANCIENT TIMES

ANCIENT EGYPTIANS USED A LANGUAGE THAT IS NO LONGER SPOKEN.

THEY HAD THEIR OWN RELIGION AND WORSHIPPED MANY GODS.

KING OF GODS
RE

Re, the sun god, was the creator of the universe and father of all the gods.

ANCIENT EGYPTIANS HAD STYLES OF DRESS ALL THEIR OWN.

THEY WORE BEAUTIFUL JEWELRY.

THEIR EYE MAKEUP WAS CALLED KOHL. IT WAS A COSMETIC AND AN ANTISEPTIC. IT MAY HAVE PROTECTED AGAINST EYE INFECTION.

We would have looked pretty funny in our modern clothes. Fortunately, I had a supply of costumes in my bag, so we looked just like the ancient Egyptians.

WHO ARE THOSE STRANGE PEOPLE?

I DON'T KNOW.

THEY SURE DON'T LOOK LIKE ANCIENT EGYPTIANS!

STYLE FROM THE NILE

CHILD'S SIDE HAIR KNOT

SOME PEOPLE SHAVED THEIR HEADS. OTHERS WORE WIGS.

ANCIENT EGYPTIANS ALSO HAD THEIR OWN STYLE OF ART. WHEN THEY DREW PICTURES OF PEOPLE, THEY COMBINED FRONT AND SIDE VIEWS. THEY THOUGHT THIS GAVE THE BEST VIEW OF EACH PART.

Head is shown from the side.

Eyes drawn as if seen from the front.

Shoulders and chest from front.

Hips, legs, and feet from side.

An ancient Egyptian town was a busy place.
Children were playing. Craftspeople were working.
We saw a bakery and a brewery in operation.
Everywhere people were buying and selling things.

My Travel Diary by Rasheeda

In the market-place we saw
- Bakers making bread from wheat and barley.
- Brewers making beer from fermented bread.
- Scribes writing down how many loaves of bread and how many jars of beer were made.
- Farmers selling animals, fruit, and vegetables.
- Craftspeople making pottery, linen cloth, sandals, baskets, and jewelry.
- Children playing many games.

BREAD BAKED IN BELL-SHAPED JARS

BEER MAKERS

SCRIBES

MIXING YEAST

FARMERS

GOD OF SCRIBES
THOTH

The god of writing was often shown as a man with an ibis head.

After school, we went home with a boy named Beku.
His father, Ramose, was a wealthy scribe
who could afford a large house.
It even had a stone bathroom where servants
poured water over their master.
This was perhaps the world's first shower!
Ramose enjoyed playing *senet* — a popular board game —
with his wife, Meryt.

Beku's family seemed busy, so we decided to leave.
On the road there was a farm family going home
from the market.
Our group didn't want to miss anything,
so we joined them.

GODDESS OF FERTILITY HATHOR

The goddess of motherhood and love was shown as a cow, or as a woman with cow's horns.

LENTILS

FLAX

FIG TREE

My Travel Diary
by Rasheeda
What farmers grew
— wheat & barley
— beans, peas, and lentils
— lettuce, cucumbers
— onions, garlic
— Melons, figs, & grapes
— Flax
(for making linen
cloth and rope)

The crops were ready to harvest.
I encouraged everyone in our group to pitch in.
We had just brought in the last of the wheat,
when the Nile started overflowing its banks.

The farmers weren't surprised when the Nile flooded.
In ancient Egypt, this happened every year.
Later, when the water drew back, it left rich mud
that fertilized the fields.
The flood made the farmers happy because it meant
good crops the next year.
It made me happy because I got to teach about it!
And it made our group happy because they love learning!

In fact, our group seemed anxious to learn about boating. I suppose they wanted to learn about traveling on the Nile. So we climbed aboard a river barge.

ALL ABOARD

BARB, DID YOU PACK OUR LIFE RAFT?

I THOUGHT YOU DID, BOB!

THIS BOAT CAN SAVE US FROM THE FLOOD.

THEN WE DON'T NEED A LIFE RAFT.

GLUG!

MEANWHILE, IN MODERN EGYPT, HERB VISITS THE ASWAN HIGH DAM...

MEDITERRANEAN SEA

GIZA • CAIRO
SINAI

EGYPT TODAY

NILE RIVER

RED SEA

LIBYA

ASWAN HIGH DAM

LAKE NASSER

SUDAN

ASWAN HIGH DAM BUILT IN THE 1960S.

IN MODERN TIMES THE NILE DOES NOT FLOOD. THIS DAM HOLDS BACK THE WATERS.

LOTSA WATER!

THIS DAM IS A HUGE ELECTRIC PLANT.

I'D RATHER HAVE THIS PLANT.

The barge was carrying stones to build a pyramid
— a tomb where an Egyptian king would be buried.
The pyramid was built in the desert.
No floodwater came there so work could go on
all year without stopping.
The ancient Egyptians had not invented wheels,
so they had to drag the stones along on the ground.

People often think the pyramids were made by slaves, but that isn't true.
Pyramid builders were paid in bread and beer, just like other workers.

Unfortunately, the pharaoh became ill at the end of the party. His wife and son helped him to bed.

The next morning there was a big commotion in the palace.
The old pharaoh had died in the night.
Everyone was weeping and wailing.

THE KING IS DEAD.

My Travel Diary
by Rasheeda
How to make a mummy
1. Remove the brain and most of the inner organs.
2. Throw the brain away.

UGH!

3. Save the inner organs in special pots called canopic jars.

Jackal=stomach   Baboon=lungs   Falcon=intestines   Human=liver

4. Pack the body with a drying salt. This stops it from rotting.

GOD OF MUMMIES
ANUBIS

The jackal-headed god, Anubis, was the protector of mummies and tombs.

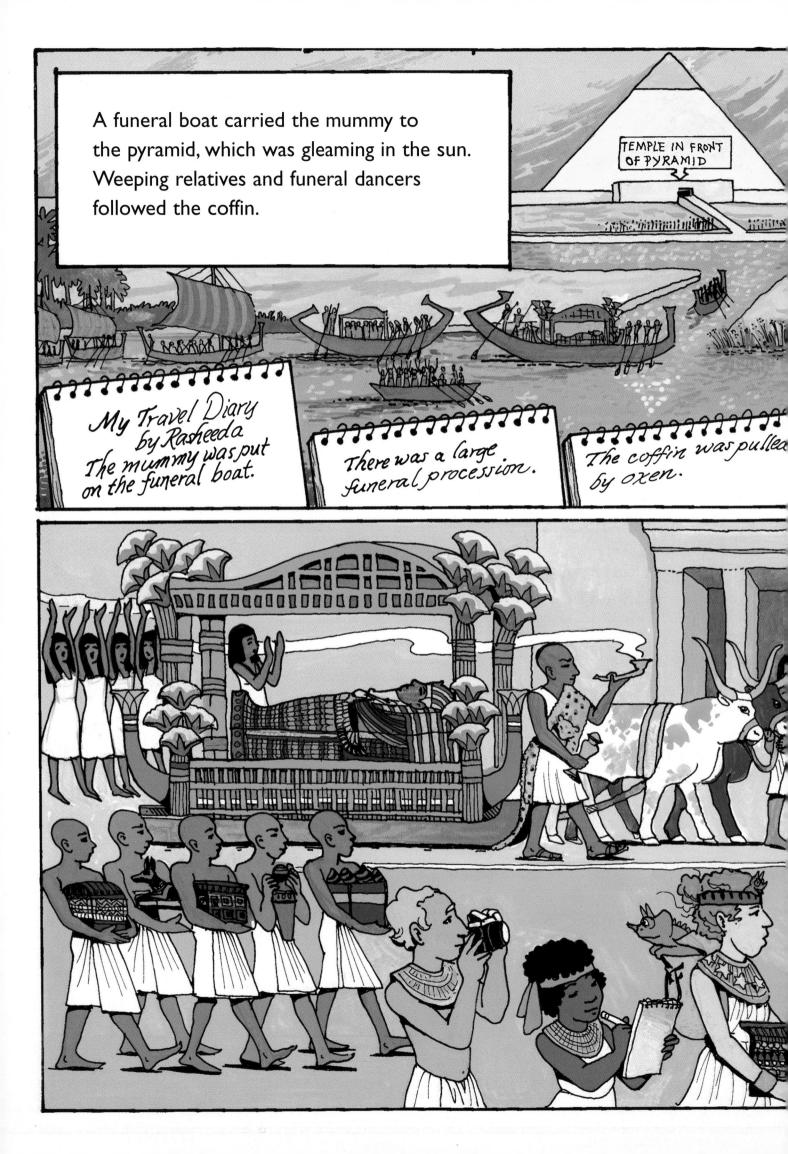

A funeral boat carried the mummy to the pyramid, which was gleaming in the sun. Weeping relatives and funeral dancers followed the coffin.

TEMPLE IN FRONT OF PYRAMID

My Travel Diary by Rasheeda
The mummy was put on the funeral boat.

There was a large funeral procession.

The coffin was pulled by oxen.

In the temple, priests performed religious ceremonies.
After the funeral, the mummy was sealed up in the pyramid.
Now the king's son would become the new pharaoh.
The old pharaoh, the Egyptians believed,
would live forever in the afterworld.

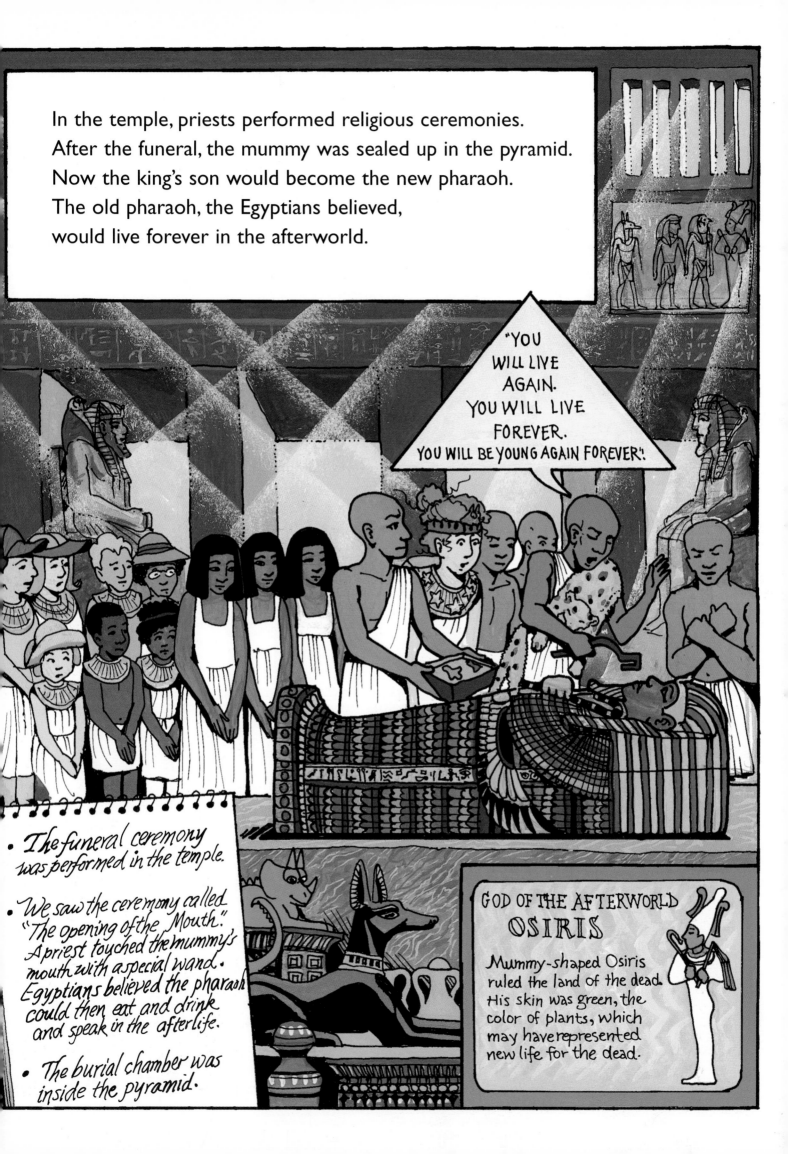

"YOU WILL LIVE AGAIN. YOU WILL LIVE FOREVER. YOU WILL BE YOUNG AGAIN FOREVER".

• The funeral ceremony was performed in the temple.

• We saw the ceremony called "The opening of the Mouth." A priest touched the mummy's mouth with a special wand. Egyptians believed the pharaoh could then eat and drink and speak in the afterlife.

• The burial chamber was inside the pyramid.

GOD OF THE AFTERWORLD
OSIRIS

Mummy-shaped Osiris ruled the land of the dead. His skin was green, the color of plants, which may have represented new life for the dead.

When the funeral was over,
a kind fisherman offered us a ride in his boat.
Along the way, things started looking pale.

By the time we reached land,
ancient Egypt was fading from sight.
(I can't imagine how that happened. Can you?)
We waved goodbye to the fisherman
and hurried to the Cairo Airport.

COULD IT REALLY HAPPEN?

If you went on a trip to Egypt, you might have many exciting adventures. But there are some things that can't happen anywhere.

FOR INSTANCE:

▲ You can't really go back in time.

▲ The door of an airplane won't open so easily, even if there is turbulence.

▲ A lizard – no matter how cute she is – does not wear clothes or act like a human in any other ways.

▲ Many events in this book could not be completed during a short school vacation. In real life, they would take months or even years.

  for example:

♦ It took ancient Egyptian embalmers seven and a half weeks to mummify a dead body.

♦ It took six months for the Nile to reach full flood stage.

♦ It took twenty years or more to build a pyramid.

▲ The pyramids were built at the beginning of ancient Egyptian history, but some of the scenes in this book are from later times, when styles were more elaborate. The pictures of the pharaoh's boat, the banquet, and the funeral all show styles that were popular thousands of years after the age of pyramids. Even though this is not really accurate in terms of time, we wanted to show readers the richness of ancient Egyptian civilization.

▲ And, last but not least, all those parachutes and stuff would never fit into one small backpack!